my astronaut helmet!

This book belongs to:

_____

a little astronaut in the making!

There was a princess called Stella, who wanted to be an astronaut.
She refused to wear her princess clothes, that the King and Queen had bought.

She would wake up every morning, put on her space helmet and suit,
then stand in front of the mirror and ask "Mummy do I look cute?"

After eating all her lunch, Stella ran upstairs to her room,

Where she had made a rocket that could fly all the way to the moon!

She sat inside her rocket, with Tink her fluffy kitten,
and they began to lift off to the solar system.

As they travelled up and up, the Earth began to shrink,
Stella was so excited but Tink was too scared to blink!

It was so FAST,
the space rocket ride,
and soon they flew past,
the clouds, the stars,
the skies.

Stella and Tink were finally in Space, a place all lit up with stars,
They stared out of the window, they could see planets,
Venus and Mars.

It was so dark, just like night,
but Space sparkled with the sun, the moon and the starlight.

Stella smiled with glee and pressed the button to fly down,
but Tink didn't like landing, she started to worry and frown.

As the rocket landed, gently on the moon,

Stella spotted an alien who looked like a cartoon!

She bounced over to the alien who was hiding behind a boulder,
and smiled in her astronaut helmet as she tapped him on his shoulder.

Patrick made a popping noise and just like magic there appeared,
a little alien spaceship, ready to be steered!

Stella, Patrick and Tink went to explore
the big planet.
Patrick took Stella to his home,
where they met his mummy, Janet.

They ate some alien jelly,
which was glittery and delicious.

Then visited a little garden, where the flowers were red and vicious.

At the end of a long day Stella hugged Patrick goodbye,
Patrick headed back home, as Stella got ready to fly.

Stella waved and promised she would be back to visit soon,
she started up the engine, and set off with a BOOM!

Tink stared from the window at all the planets and stars,
and began to yawn, she was tired, and it was dark.

Stella landed the rocket carefully back
in her play room,
then took off her space helmet and her
astronaut costume.

So tired and cosy, all tucked up in her warm bed,
the King and Queen came in, to kiss Stella on the head.

From the window she could see all the bright stars gleaming,
and finally off to sleep, Stella started dreaming.